By Lydia Lukidis
Illustrated by André Ceolin

Kane Press
New York

To all the children I meet during my workshops and readings, thank you for inspiring me and reminding me why I love my job!—L.L.

To Gabriel and Grace, for their patience and support.—A.C.

Special thanks to beekeeping expert Kelsey Ducsharm for her help with the manuscript and the art.

Library of Congress Cataloging-in-Publication Data
Names: Lukidis, Lydia, author. | Ceolin, André, illustrator.
Title: The broken bees' nest / by Lydia Lukidis ; illustrated by André Ceolin.
Description: New York : Kane Press, 2019. | Series: Makers make it work |
Summary: When Arun and Keya find a beehive that is caving in, they ask their neighbor, Dr. Chen, who is a beekeeper, for help.
Identifiers: LCCN 2018022818 | ISBN 9781635921137 (pbk) | ISBN 9781635921120 (reinforced library binding) | ISBN 9781635921144 (ebook)
Subjects: | CYAC: Honeybee—Fiction. | Bee culture—Fiction. |
Brothers and sisters—Fiction.
Classification: LCC PZ7.1.L845 Bro 2019 | DDC [E]—dc23
LC record available at https://lccn.loc.gov/2018022818

10 9 8 7 6 5 4 3 2 1

First published in the United States of America in 2019 by Kane Press, Inc.
Printed in China

Book Design: Michelle Martinez

Arun and his little sister, Keya, scouted the forest trail.

"What about this one?" Keya asked.

Arun checked out the tree. "Too small."

He was looking for the perfect tree. His father had promised to build them a tree house that ummer!

Arun stopped by a big oak tree. "Wowza!" he said. "This is it!"

Keya paused. "What's that sound?"

They both looked up. A bee's nest hung from one of the branches. A swarm of angry-looking bees was flying around it.

"BEES!" Keya cried. "Run for your life!"

Arun grabbed her hand. "They won't hurt you if you don't bother them. Bees are totally amazing. I learned all about them at summer camp."

Did you know that honeybees help our food grow? They move pollen from one part of a plant to another. That's what makes seeds for new plants!

Arun took a closer look at the bees. Their nest didn't look right. One side was falling off the branch.

"Their home is coming apart," he said. "We should help them."

"No way," Keya said. "It's too dangerous. We're not bee experts."

That gave Arun an idea. "That's it! Let's go see Dr. Chen! She'll know what to do."

Dr. Chen lived down the road. She had a beehive in her backyard and sold honey at the farmers market.

Arun checked with their parents first. When their dad said yes, they raced to Dr. Chen's house. The whole way, Arun kept thinking about the bees. What if he couldn't help them?

Beekeeping is when people keep and take care of honeybees. Beekeepers collect the honey and beeswax that the bees make.

Arun and Keya found Dr. Chen in the backyard.

"You're just in time," she said. "I need another set of hands. Can you hold this box steady?" She nodded at a wooden box next to her.

Arun carefully held the box while Dr. Chen hammered in five nails. Then she picked up another piece of wood. "Keya, will you place this on top?"

Dr. Chen screwed hinges on. "There," she said. "It's done!"

"What is it?" Arun asked.

"It's my new beehive." Dr. Chen brushed her hands on her jeans. "Now, what can I do for you?"

"We found a nest in the forest," Arun said. "But something's wrong with it. The bees are swarming around! They look scared!"

Dr. Chen straightened up. "We'd better check it out!"

Keya frowned. "Arun, do we have to? I don't want to get stung."

Safety first!
Beekeepers wear special one-piece suits to protect themselves. They also wear hats with veils that cover their heads.

"You'll be safe with these," Dr. Chen said.

She stuffed three funny-looking suits into a large backpack. Then she dropped a hat on Keya's head and one on Arun's. Veils hung in front of their faces.

Arun led Dr. Chen through the woods to the tree.

Dr. Chen studied it. “Yep,” she said. “This comb has been damaged, no doubt about it. It was probably destroyed by a raccoon. Those rascals love honey! In any case, the bees need a new home, right away. The queen bee looks upset.”

Keya perked up. "Queen bee? Is she really a queen?"

"You bet," Dr. Chen said. "She doesn't wear a crown, but she's the leader of the colony."

A *colony* is a family of bees. It can have thousands of bees! But each colony has only one queen bee.

Dr. Chen opened her bag. "The bees can use my new beehive. You kids want to help?"

Arun nodded. Keya wasn't so sure.

"Keya, don't you want to save the queen bee?" Arun asked. "Then we can go back to planning our tree house."

"We'll be safe in our beekeeper gear," Dr. Chen said. "BEE-lieve me!"

Keya smiled. "Okay."

Dr. Chen helped the kids put on beekeeping suits. Arun and Keya giggled.

"I feel like a spaceman," Arun said.

"Time for Operation Bee Free!" Dr. Chen brought out a bee smoker. "We'll use smoke to calm the bees. Arun, want to try?"

She showed Arun how to squeeze the bellows on the smoker. The smoke spread. Already the bees seemed calmer.

Fire drill! If bees smell smoke, they gobble honey to get ready to look for a new home. When their bellies grow, it's hard for them to use their stingers. Then beekeepers can more safely approach the hive.

Dr. Chen found the queen bee. She helped her into a special box Keya held.

Soon, the other bees followed.

Then Dr. Chen packed up a piece of the nest that wasn't damaged. "This is for us," she said. "It's filled with honey!"

Keya's eyes lit up. "Can we have some?"

"You bet!" Dr. Chen said. "But first we need to get these bees to their new home."

They took the bees to Dr. Chen's backyard. Arun opened the box. A bee came out and flew in circles.

"She looks happy," Keya said.

"Yep," Dr. Chen said. "Bees dance to show other bees where to find flowers!" She carefully placed all the bees inside the wooden beehive. "We just have to see if the colony takes to its new home."

"I hope so!" Arun said.

"Now for the best part," said Dr. Chen. "Time to get the honey!"

She placed the piece of old nest on her workbench and took out the honeycomb.

Ever wonder what a honeycomb is? It's a collection of many six-sided wax cells. The bees store their pollen, eggs, and honey inside.

"Ready to get sticky?" Dr. Chen asked.

Arun and Keya used wooden spoons to mash up the honeycomb. Dr. Chen put the pieces into a strainer. Slowly, pure honey oozed out.

Dr. Chen handed Arun and Keya spoons. "Try some."

"It's BEE-licious!" Keya said.

"Let's fill some jars for the market," said Dr. Chen.

People have been eating honey for thousands of years! In Egypt, honey was even found in the pyramids.

She brought out six jars. Keya washed and dried them carefully. Dr. Chen showed Arun how to pour the honey into the jars. Once a jar was full, Arun wiped the edge with a damp cloth. He placed a lid on top and twisted it tight.

Then Keya stuck labels on the jars.

"Can we come by sometime to help with the new beehive?" she asked.

Dr. Chen winked at them. "You bet!"

On the way home, they couldn't stop talking about the bees.

"Are they going to be happy there?" Keya asked.

"I think so," Arun said. "They'll be a lot safer from raccoons."

Keya was quiet for a minute. Then she asked, "Will they mind us using their old home for our tree house?"

Arun thought about Keya's question all night. He couldn't sleep, so he crept out of bed. He knew just what to do. He had a surprise for his sister.

The next day, his mom had a surprise of her own. "We'll start building the tree house today!"

Arun's dad packed a toolbox and a picnic basket. Arun packed his surprise for Keya in his backpack.

Then the whole family trooped through the woods to the oak tree.

"What's for lunch?" Keya asked.

"Dr. Chen stopped by this morning," their mom said. "The bees like their new beehive. She also gave me a jar of honey you two helped with. So we made cheese and honey sandwiches!"

"Wowza!" Arun said. Now was the perfect time for his surprise.

He pulled a wooden sign from his backpack.

"First, I came up with a name for our tree house—the Beehive!"

He hung the sign from one of the branches.

Their mom whistled. Their dad whooped. Keya clapped loudly.

"Plus, the Beehive needs a queen bee. A queen is brave enough to help a colony even when she's a little afraid." Arun reached into his backpack again and pulled out . . .

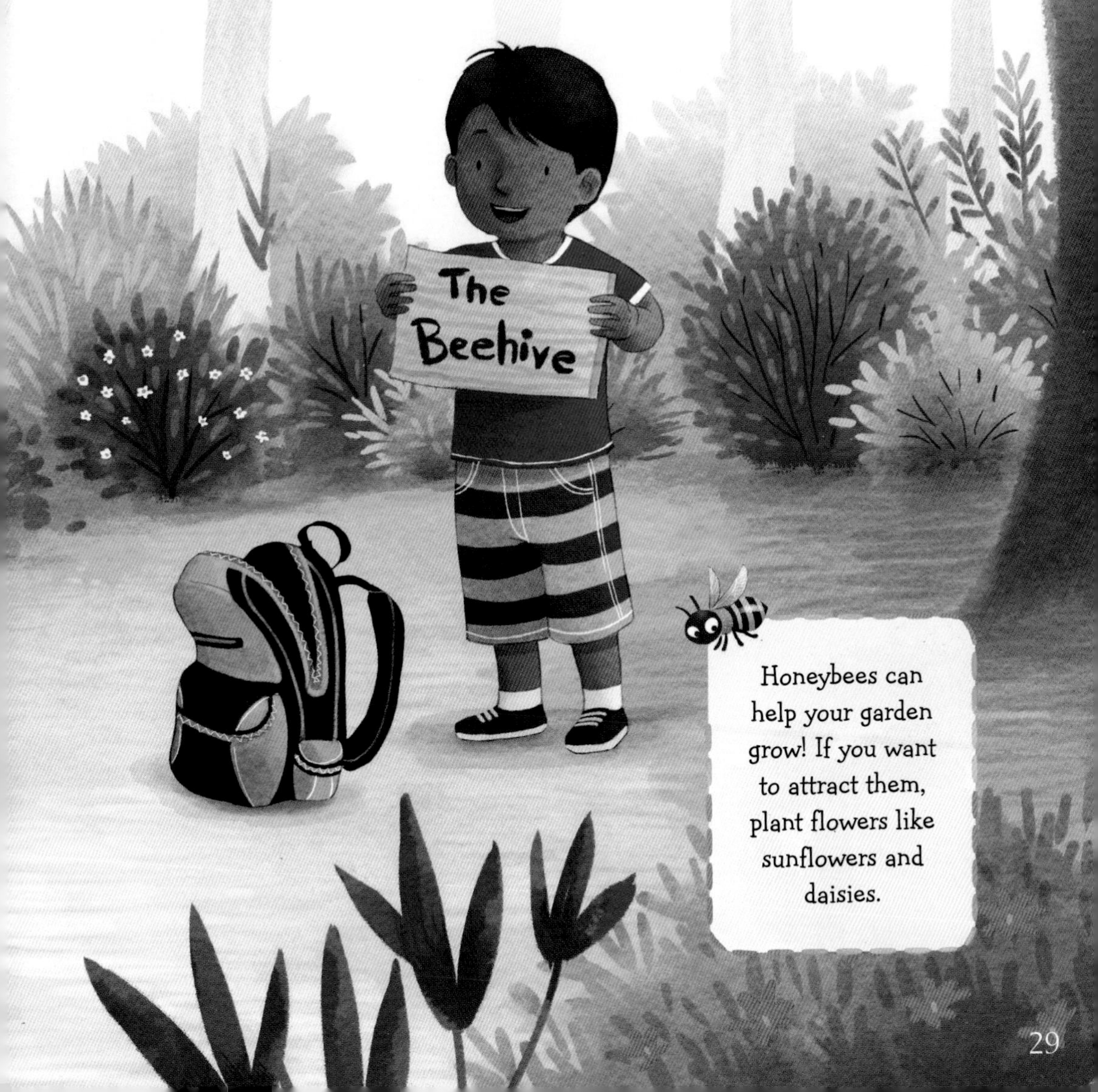
The Beehive
Honeybees can help your garden grow! If you want to attract them, plant flowers like sunflowers and daisies.

A crown!

He placed it on his sister's head. "Let's hear it for Keya the Queen Bee!"

Keya's smile couldn't have been any bigger. "Here's my honey dance!" she said. She danced in circles like a bee.

And not far over her head, a honeybee buzzed in circles, too.

Learn Like a Maker

When Arun found a damaged bees' nest, he wanted to help! Luckily, he knew just the person to ask. With Dr. Chen, he found the bees a new home—and got a very sweet reward!

Look Back

- On pages 16–19, Dr. Chen, Arun, and Keya moved the bees. How did they get them to the new hive?
- Look back at pages 28–31. How did Keya feel when Arun surprised her with the sign and crown? How do you know?

Try This!

Be a Friend to Bees

You can help bees by planting a bee-friendly garden! Bees like three kinds of flowers best:

- Flowers with a good area for bees to land
- Tube-shaped flowers
- Flowers with spikes

At a local garden store, look for seeds for these kinds of flowers. Find a nice spot to plant them, in your backyard or in a pot. When the flowers grow, watch for bees!

TIP: Did you know that bees can't see the color red? Blue, purple, and yellow flowers catch their attention better! Try wild lilac in the spring, bee balm in the summer, and zinnias in the fall.